Fuzzy

a twisted cryptid novella

Roni Stinger

Stinger Stories

Contents

Prologue

Crickets sang to their potential mates in the provincial park forest. In the full moonlight, Mark Miller didn't need the headlamp he wore, but it would come in handy once he and Sandy were inside the hot springs cave. He didn't want to miss a second of Sandy's sexy body or any additional skin off his shins. The rocks had a habit of grabbing a taste of flesh if you weren't careful.

About a kilometer left to hike, Sandy snuggled into the crook of his muscular arm, the forest path unfolded. He'd been hitting the weights all winter, excited to show off his efforts come springtime. Now he'd have a chance.

"What about bears...mountain lions? Is it safe?" Sandy shivered in the crisp spring air, folding her arms across her chest, enhancing her cleavage.

Her raven curls hung below her shoulders. Mark had no doubt she was ready for him. There was a certain way women walked when they were ready. His dad told him that. Sandy had that walk.

"The team doesn't call me Macho Mark for being a chickenshit."

Steam tendrils rose in the distance, reaching towards the sky. Silhouettes of trees and bushes lined the trail. A rustling, crunching, whoosh interrupted the horny cricket chirps. Sandy stopped. Mark nearly tripped over her. Rolling around in the dirt would be fun, but better to warm her up in the springs first if he didn't want her getting squeamish.

"Mark?" Sandy pointed into the trees. "Did you hear that?"

She stepped back. The crickets went silent.

"I don't—"

A dark shape swooped down from a giant evergreen. Sandy let out a squeak of a scream, covering her head. They'd all heard stories about bats getting caught in someone's hair.

Just last year, Dionne's cousin's friend got one stuck in her hair while rowing around Lake Louise. Whole colony flew over the boat. Missed everyone but her. While the bat struggled to get untangled, the girl panicked, fell off the boat, and drowned. Locals say you can still hear her screaming at dusk. Whether true or not, a story like that stuck with a person.

The little black demon flew in a circle above. Mark let out his breath with a slight chuckle. He wasn't afraid of no bat. Besides, he'd traded in his mullet for a short spikey cut this year.

"Come on. That nosy lady warden is just looking for someone to fine." Mark grabbed Sandy's hand.

With the bat a safe distance away, Sandy smiled.

"Quit talking." She planted a kiss on his lips, ducked and ran.

The trail opened to a bubbling spring at the base of a rocky hill, lit in moonlight. The cave entrance merged with the darkness at the edge of the springs that butted against the rock, but Mark knew where to find the opening. Hadn't failed to find one yet, even in the dark.

Yellow caution tape disturbed the fairy tale image. It ringed the pool, a new addition since Mark had snuck in last summer. On that trip, he'd never made it to the water before ol' iron tits warden caught him. This time, he'd left his truck down the road from the parking lot, hoping she wouldn't hear or see him. No reason for her to be out at this time of night, but you never knew. The lady was a strange one.

"Woah, this is amazing." Sandy bent down and pulled off her boots. "Why'd they close it anyhow?"

Mark shushed her. Giving Mark a quick smile over her shoulder before entering the water, she jumped out of her clothes. Obviously, she'd done this sort of thing a few times before. He'd bought her a dollar rose at the gas station on the way and she'd been as grateful as if he'd bought her a diamond ring. His kind of girl. Cheap and easy.

Her boobs glistened in the moonlight.

"Ah, it's so nice! What are you waiting for?"

Mark, wearing nothing but his headlamp and a smile, didn't let that caution tape slow him down any more than Sandy had.

The hot waters enveloped their bodies, soothing every bit of skin. Mark inhaled the steam, warming his lungs. There was nothing better than that first plunge. His dick grew hard in anticipation.

Sandy dipped lower into the water as she entered the cave. Mark didn't want to lose her in the darkness but didn't want to turn on his headlamp yet. If he did, they'd risk alerting the warden by shining their presence outside. Her cabin wasn't too far as the crow flies, and she really was out for him.

She'd caught him sneaking around on a few occasions. Besides, she might mention the other girls to Sandy. That wouldn't help him out any. Once he and Sandy were far enough inside the cavern, he'd turn on the light without worrying about the old lady.

He grabbed Sandy and pulled her behind him. That would earn him points. Chicks loved hiding behind their men. He felt his way along the curvature of the rock wall, slick and smooth with steam. He caressed the wall with his free hand. Delicious.

"Stop it, Mark. That tickles." Sandy slapped his arm.

"What—" As he turned toward her, he smacked his shin on a protruding rock. "Shit! Ow, that fucking hurt!"

He let go of Sandy's hand and reached down to assess the injury. A couple centimeters deep divot nested into his calf. Mineral water stung the open wound.

"Sandy?" Mark heard her splash. "Wait for me."

How the hell had she gotten in front of him?

"Mark, stop. That hurt." Sandy's voice echoed off the cavern walls, a couple of meters away.

Absolute darkness rendered Mark's hand invisible when he held it in front of his face. Hopefully, they were far enough inside now. Either way, he had to do it.

He turned on his headlamp. The cave walls were coated in salmon-colored slime. Stalactites hung from the ceiling like swords centimeters above Mark's head. He hadn't realized how close he'd been to spiking his brain. Good damned thing he wasn't any taller. Obscured by steam, the light illuminated only a short distance. Anything farther than a half-meter away was nothing more than white billows.

"Sandy?" She couldn't have gone far.

The water ahead churned in agitation.

He stepped forward.

"What the fu—" Sandy's scream went silent as if submerged by water.

"Sandy?" Mark's heart raced, panic spreading through every nerve.

He put his hands out, searching for her. Empty air. More splashing ahead. The water bloomed with red bubbles. Something scraped his leg. Sharp. Biting.

"What the—"

Mark tried to run, slamming into the rock wall. His headlamp, knocked from his head, sank to the bottom, briefly illuminating a swirling blue-green mass that engulfed the red, leaving clear water in its wake. Mark didn't understand what he was seeing. Still, those stinging bites lit his skin on fire. If only he had his hockey stick, he'd fight back. His naked body assured him he had no weapons.

Slow and awkward, legs and torso covered with needle-like punctures, he attempted to escape. Tingling and numbness spread from each tiny prick. His legs wouldn't obey his command to run. Catching his left calf with his right foot, he slipped beneath the swirls of red and blue-green.

Rising again, he gasped for breath. He had nearly reached the cave's opening. The full moon, bright in the night sky, offered hope. Stupid water bugs, or whatever they were, wouldn't be the end of him. He lunged for the light, moving as if in a dream. A clump of red, oozing tissue stuck to his arm. Globs of flesh and fat in shades of pink and yellow floated atop the water, whether from him or Sandy, he wasn't sure. This wasn't his lucky night.

He pulled through the water with both arms. Those fiery pinpricks crawled up his neck. He screamed. His vision went dark.

Clawing at his face, the pain unbearable, Mark fell beneath the water for the last time.

Chapter One

The sun had barely risen, churning the sky hues of orange and pink, as Jamie Mathers soothed her skin and aching joints. She'd soaked here nearly every morning since getting her position as the warden in charge. The screech of a Clark's nutcracker, shriek of an upset chipmunk, and birdsong created an orchestra of nature.

The grotto was gloriously peaceful since officials closed the hot spring after a little shaker last year. 4.0 on the Richter scale. The earthquake hadn't been a big one, but destabilizing, nonetheless. Inspections of the cave afterwards showed the rocks had shifted. Park services couldn't risk the liability of someone getting hurt.

Jamie preferred soaking outside the cave, too claustrophobic inside. Her little cabin, a kilometer from the hot springs, gave her easy access, allowing her to make sure no one loitered in the closed area. A rest from having to give tours and deal with tourists on the daily granted Jamie's greatest wish. All she had to do was turn people away and keep it all to herself. Working with the public was a sure way to grow a desire for solitude. Now she had it. Except for Aaron, but he barely counted. He did his work and left her alone for the most part. A quiet kid, obsessed with folklore and monsters. She even enjoyed working with him on projects. Kind of liked his company.

A finch landed beside the bank. Its scarlet breast and head bright against brown and white wings. Scratching along the hardened earth, the bird pecked for insects and seeds, to no avail. Settling on a tiny piece of gravel or two, it lifted its beak and swallowed. Hopping into the water, it preened, lifting a wing to wash its head and neck.

Considered a holy place by early people, legends said the springs had once been inhabited by all types of creatures. Predators and prey soaked peacefully together at the grotto.

Jamie had never taken to religion, but these waters were surely the only thing she'd found worthy of worship. She'd made the right decision moving to Canada from Kansas after her father had died.

Freshly thawed earth, the first blooms of spring lilies, and pine wafted on the gentle morning breeze. Sulphur, like a stale old fart, rose from the pool. Filled by dozens of thermal vents beneath the bedrock, the cold mountain temperatures cooled the soaking pool to a perfect forty degrees Celsius. The cave ran a couple degrees hotter.

Old growth fir, spruce, and aspens stood guard in the surrounding forest. Indian paintbrush, yarrow, and columbine thrived in the undergrowth, throwing their reds, yellows, and whites into the forest green. There was nothing like it in Kansas. Flat fields and wide-open skies were the lands she grew up in. Hard to believe it'd been thirty years since she'd left.

An object bobbed in the water near the cave opening. Squinting without her glasses, she didn't recognize the shape. Hopefully, another animal hadn't drowned. Seemed to be happening more and more, recently. Last week, she fetched two birds and a bat from the water. Poor things, but dead was dead, nothing to do but dispose of them. The damage had been done. Last thing she needed were carcasses contaminating her springs.

She stood, wading through the hip deep water. Drawing closer to the object, a mixture of white, pink, red, and yellow tissue evident, the shape remained a mystery. If it was an animal, it had been stripped of fur or feathers.

Something was attached to the object. Large, floating just beneath the surface, flesh shreds hanging from bone. The shape of the first object finally made sense. A foot. A goddamn human foot. The rest of the body, attached by nothing but bone at the ankle. Jesus Christ. What happened here? There was barely anything left.

As she tried to understand what she was seeing, another body, in similar shape, bobbed to the surface. Tendons, ligaments, and muscle hung from bones in strips and strings. Jamie gagged. Turning away, she counted slowly to five and regained her composure. Whatever happened to these two was unlike anything she'd seen. Poor things. The organs were gone. Nothing but fleshy empty rib cages torn asunder. White ligaments bright against the mass of mutilated flesh and fat. Goddammit, this was the last thing she needed.

The authorities would shut the springs down for sure. People should just stay the hell out, and things like this wouldn't happen. They'd all been warned. A cave in, maybe, but that didn't explain the damage to their bodies. What kind of mess had they gotten into to end up like that? Damage wasn't from a fall injury. A wild animal attack? But what kind of animal did something like that? None, that's what kind, at least not around here.

The authorities would be all over her park looking for answers, probably kill a dozen innocent bears and mountain lions, just in case.

Two years ago, a guy had stored food in his tent against park orders. Bears dragged him out and helped themselves to the banquet. Guess the guy's supplies weren't enough, because they finished the guy off too. Took him into the woods, and whatever the bear didn't finish, the crows, eagles, and vultures took care of. Nothing much but bones when the warden found him. Those bones had obvious signs of bear and bird damage, unlike these ones. They ended up killing two sows and three cubs before officials found evidence. A watch and a partially digested hand in the last sow's belly.

The kids were already dead. She didn't want the authorities crawling all over the place, stomping on her fragile spring buds, muddying up the springs, and murdering animals.

Blobs of flesh floated around her. She didn't want to be in the water for another second, yet her legs didn't want to carry her out either. Almost like they were glued to the rocky bottom. Finally, they obeyed orders, and she waded out of the pool in her skivvies. Shivering in the morning chill, she pulled her pants, shirt, and jacket on. In the bushes, a burst of color caught her attention. A red shirt.

She pulled on her boots and walked over to investigate. Two haphazard piles of belongings lay to the side of the trail leading in. She hadn't noticed them in her haste to enter the healing water this morning.

She pulled her leather work gloves from her jacket pocket and put them on. Tentatively, she picked up the red shirt. Beneath it lay a pair of denim jeans, tighty-whities, and a jacket. No way they walked here, but she hadn't heard or seen any vehicles. Searching the pockets of the jeans and jacket, she found a wallet and condoms, but no keys. A pair of size twelve boots sat off to the side.

Jamie opened the wallet. Mark Miller, she knew the name as soon as she saw his face. She'd chased him off a few times. Sometimes saw his family in town. Dad was some big shot, but Jamie didn't care about that sort of thing. Shit, knowing the kid, even though she'd never liked him, made this all a lot harder. Mark always had some girl or another with him. Maybe he'd let her drive, or she took his keys to make sure she didn't get stranded.

Jamie steeled herself before searching the next pile. She lifted the girl's blouse, examining the pink rose bud fabric. No place to hide keys there. She pushed the girl's panties aside and searched her jean pockets. Nothing. Not that it was surprising. Girls' pants never had deep enough pockets to hold anything. That's why Jamie had always bought men's jeans.

As soon as she picked up the girl's puffy coat the jingle gave her hope. Sure enough, lip gloss, photo ID, and the keys fell into Jamie's hand as she shook out the pockets. Pretty girl, but Jamie didn't recognize the face on her ID. The girl had been smart to keep the keys. That Jamie respected. She felt sorry for the girl for a moment, but the girl didn't have anything to worry about anymore. That wasn't such a bad thing.

The girl's long dark hair fanned out like a palm frond in the wind atop the water. It reminded Jamie of her own hair back in high school, before she'd cut it short, the way she liked. Jamie looked around nervously, making sure no one was watching. Time and space narrowed.

No time for dawdling, she'd have to find Mark's truck and take care of the bodies before Aaron got up. No one else should be around for a while. Jamie needed to fish those bodies out and hide them temporarily, just in case. Not the kind of thing she'd want Aaron to stumble upon.

After she looked for the vehicle, she'd do something more permanent with the bodies. She scoured the surrounding area for a long stick, preferably one with a cross branch. Not finding anything sufficient, she broke a two-meter branch off a pine tree and cut all but two of its cross branches off. No matter which way it turned, it would have a nice hook.

Mark floated closer to the shoreline. The slight wave from the breeze pushed flesh streamers back and forth. Kneeling at the water's edge she hooked the stick below his chin, focusing on the tiny bubbles released from fissures below. She grabbed his upper arm bone and pulled. Thankfully, there was enough connective tissue left for the rest of his body to follow.

Dragging him into the thick brush far enough to be out of sight, she threw small branches and needles over him for camouflage. Then, she went back for the girl. The stick barely reached her. There was less of the girl to snag. Jamie tried to tangle the stick in the girl's hair, but it kept pulling loose.

On the third attempt, she caught beneath the girl's arm bone, pulling her half a meter before the stick let go. Another chunk of flesh tore loose from her arm, bobbing along the shoreline like fish chum. The healthy population of eagles, vultures, and coyotes might help her out. Otherwise, pulling out all those pieces wouldn't be fun.

Hooking the girl again, she almost made it to shore before the stick slipped loose. Jamie reached out with her gloved hand, gripping the girl's hair. As she pulled, she twisted the strands into her fist. The girl's body scraped along the rocks, leaving a few chunks of fresh wet flesh behind.

After hiding the girl in the brush, Jamie grabbed the clothes and tied them in a bundle onto her bike. She had a couple of hours to take care of things. Everything should be nice and quiet until then.

Bright red flashes peeked through the trees as Jamie bounced down the old forest road, leaving the lower parking lot. As she grew closer, the red flashes clarified into the shape of a pickup truck. Not just any truck. She'd have recognized the Miller boy's Ford anywhere.

She leaned her bike against the big spruce log she and Aaron had downed across the road last fall. It had been Aaron's first week on the job. His idea to fell the tree to stop trespassers. It'd already been dead from a lightning strike last year, so using it to discourage people from sneaking into the springs sounded like a great idea. It stopped most of them.

They'd parked the truck on the cliff side of the road. The easiest thing would be to roll it off, but someone would find it and be looking for bodies. Jamie circled the truck.

Two sets of boot tracks led towards the road. By the looks of them, it had been a few hours, which would have put the kids here well before sunrise. Dragging her boot across the mud, she covered the tracks.

Kids disappeared from these small towns all the time. They got lost in the woods or ran off to bigger cities and dreams. Sure, their parents would look, but everyone would whisper that the kids had run off, maybe eloped even, especially if they never found the vehicle. That would be a sure sign they were a couple of runaways. If they were over eighteen, they could leave if they wanted. Hell, even at sixteen, no one would spend too much time worrying about their whereabouts. It's the way of teenagers.

Jamie had a place in mind to ditch the truck. Somewhere no one would find it. An old forest road with too many porcupines. They'd eat off your tires before you hiked a kilometer away. Too much hassle to put wire fences around your vehicle for a day hike, and if you were gone longer than a day, those porcupines would eat through the fences too. Nice dense brush in the area. She threw her bike in the back of the truck. Keys in the ignition, it started on the first try.

Jamie drove far enough to avoid accidental visitors, then off-road, into the brush, as far as the truck would take her. The undergrowth, taller than the hood, caused the tires to spin. This would be its final resting place. She gathered branches and leaves and threw them atop the truck for good measure.

It wouldn't take long to bike back to the springs. The game trails cut a straight shot. All the miles of cycling and hard work kept her in relatively excellent physical condition. Despite her rheumatism diagnosis last year her health got better with every soak. She'd need to hurry if she wanted to get this done before Aaron was up. Moments like this made her wish the powers-that-be hadn't made her take him on, but they'd decided it wasn't good for her to be here for months alone. Although that was exactly why she'd taken the job.

The game trail, overgrown with thick vegetation along the sides, narrowed to a single track, slowing her. The deer and elk hadn't been active enough to trample it down well. She forced herself to keep peddling past the early season bear grass blooms and the wild irises pushing through the soil. For a moment, in the glory of nature, she almost forgot about the bodies. Almost. It wasn't the sort of thing you forgot easily. The Three Sisters mountains in the west shimmered in the sun. She'd almost reached the main entrance road. A car door slammed in the distance. Better to head them off than have them wander to the springs.

She pedaled as hard and fast as her legs would go.

CHAPTER TWO

Jamie smelled the sheriff before she saw him. Sickeningly sweet aroma of tobacco. Then the disgusting squish of spit as it hit her pristine forest floor. Sheriff Anders paced the area, wad of chew tucked into his lower lip, buzzcut hidden below his hat, looking at the ground.

"Howdy, sheriff." She brushed her gloves on the thighs of her pants for effect. "Doing a little road maintenance."

He had a way of looking at her that said she was too old to fuck and not man enough to take seriously. Pissed her off, but she preferred it to the looks men like him offered when she was a young woman.

"Well, we got a couple of kids missing. Looks like some fresh car tracks on the road."

Goddammit, she didn't need this right now.

"Damn, sheriff." She gave him her most concerned look. "Never saw a vehicle. If they were here, must've already left."

"Hmm." The sheriff rubbed his chin. "Either way, I think I'll take a look around." He pushed by her and headed up the road towards the springs.

The sheriff walked the perimeter of the hot pool, looking for tracks. He wouldn't find any. Stone and hard packed silt surrounded the pool. The morning sun had dried up the last dribbles of water left from dragging out the bodies. The rest of the tracks Jamie had obliterated. The sheriff bent down and put his hand in the springs.

"Kids like this stuff, huh? Feels slimy to me. Stuff floating in it too."

Oh shit. She'd forgotten about the kid pieces. The sheriff's gaze moved towards the waterline where white sediment and algae floated. Thank goodness. Jamie scanned and found a few dried clumps along the shore.

"Never understood the draw." He stood, shaking the water off his hand. "Maybe they got themselves home by now." He rested his hands on his hips, stretching his back.

The couple of broken limbs through the brush stuck out to Jamie, but the sheriff wouldn't notice. He'd transferred from the city a couple of years back and still had no idea what he was doing in the woods. From the way Jamie heard, it was the only position that would take him after what had happened. He'd shot a few holes in the ceiling of his home while arguing with his ex-wife. Seems Sheriff Anders had a problem with alcohol, but that didn't matter too much around here. As long as he stayed sober on the job, no one much cared.

"Hope so, sheriff. There's lots of woods to get lost in." Jamie shook her head. "Last thing we need is more trouble in the park."

She didn't need more altercations with the sheriff, either. They didn't see eye to eye on most things, but she tried to keep things cordial between them. He was a land use man, and she was a conservationist. Still, they were on the same team, protecting the park and its residents.

Sheriff Anders tipped his hat.

"That's one thing we agree on, Jamie. Doesn't do any of us any good to have trouble in the park. I'm hoping the deer numbers will be high enough next year to open for a season." He turned and walked down the trail before she responded.

All Jamie's muscles tightened as she clenched her jaw. Laws protected wildlife in the park, but occasionally, authorities opened for hunting to control the deer population. Far as she was concerned, it wasn't the deer numbers that were out of control, it was men like the sheriff.

Still, that didn't stop people from trying to hunt out of season now and then. Sometimes she found evidence. Zero tolerance for that sort of thing meant hefty fines and possible jail time. It didn't take much to discourage those who just figured they'd get away with it.

Jamie let out a long exhale once the sheriff was out of sight. Despite the hunting comment, the conversation had gone pretty well, but he'd eaten away more of her limited time. There was no way to get the bodies buried before Aaron might be up.

In the distance, the crunch of bicycle tires drifted her way, growing louder. Aaron.

Early season run-off had already breached the creek's bank on the west end and done damage to the surrounding flora. They'd need to shore up the land before the big thaw. Perfect. That would keep Aaron away from the springs for a while. She biked down the road, intercepting Aaron on his way toward her cabin.

He sat on his bike, looking like a model straight out of some fancy men's magazine, except for the flannel shirt and work gloves. She never figured out how he stayed looking so nice.

"Morning, Jamie." He flashed her his big grin.

Perfect white teeth, a testament to his privileged upbringing. Despite all that, she liked him. He reminded her of her kid brother.

A bitter-sweet memory, thanks to the tractor accident. She imagined he'd have looked a lot like Aaron, minus the metro model thing, if he'd have lived long enough to become an adult. Probably would have stayed on the farm and raised little grandbaby farmers like Dad had always wanted.

She wasn't in the mood for pleasantries.

"Need to shore up the creek today, Aaron."

"Sounds good. Gotta get my exercise for the day." Aaron made a muscle man pose and laughed.

Jamie ignored his joke, still pondering what little Jonny might have grown up to be. She found herself easily distracted these days.

"The ground's nice and soft. Should make the job pretty easy. I've got some cleanup to do in the parking area. Kids were up partying again." Dammit, why had she said that, among all the excuses she might have chosen?

"You catch em?" The smile disappeared off Aaron's face and a hint of a crease that would surely grow into a groove over the next decade appeared between his eyes.

"Nah, probably stopped to make out in the parking lot. Left a few beer cans and butts." She hadn't seen any such thing, but it was believable enough.

"Fucking kids, screw things up for everyone," Aaron said.

Funny Aaron saying something like that when he was only a few years older than those kids. He seemed different, though. Serious, responsible, and respectful. He always got his duties done before heading out to explore the trails, never screwed off during work hours. Didn't seem interested in hanging out with the locals either, which was the biggest plus for Jamie. She didn't need a bunch of folks dropping by for visits.

"I'll be down to help when I'm done. We should be able to finish in a couple of days." Jamie smiled, hoping it looked natural because it felt anything but.

"All righty, then. Be careful. Heard on my scanner about another sasquatch sighting last night," Aaron said.

"Ah, I'm not scared of your sasquatch. Spent too much time in the woods to worry about that."

Aaron laughed and nodded.

"See ya later." He waved and headed up the trail.

Things were nice and easy with Aaron. Too bad everyone wasn't like him. Just doing their damn jobs and mind-ing their own business. Too many people wanted to be in everyone else's business.

Jamie biked back to the springs, leaving Aaron to do his work. If she left the bodies for too long, the animals might get them, but she needed a few supplies from the cabin first. The small log home was the sort of thing she'd always dreamed of. Nothing fancy. One bedroom with a couple of folding chairs sitting on the little front porch. The simple furnishings came with the place and were nicely accented by the few personal items Jamie owned. Books. Magazines. An old black-and-white picture of her mom and dad. Full color family photo taken just before her mom's death from cancer.

Jamie was around twelve in the picture. Her brother Jonny would have been eight. The little bible she'd kept from her first stay in a city hotel sat next to the picture. She grabbed the bible. Wouldn't hurt to read a passage to send off the kids. She wasn't especially religious, but it felt like the right thing to do. She'd give them a decent burial. No reason more harm needed to be done.

The kids were dead, finding them in their current condition wouldn't bring comfort to anyone. She was doing the family a favor, really.

After putting the bible in her pocket, she went out to the utility shed at the end of her drive. Tying a tarp on the rack on her bike, she grabbed a shovel from the cluttered shed and slung it over one shoulder. Steering with her other hand, she rode back to deal with the bodies.

As she pulled up to the springs, a young red fox pranced away from the bodies, carrying a human femur. Son-of-a-bitch. It was too late.

Jamie hopped off her bike and shouted, "Drop it!"

The animals in this area were usually quite skittish since there weren't many visitors. No such luck with the fox. He refused to drop his prize, even though the large bone slowed him to a walk. He tried to escape. A flash of magenta lit Jamie's mind. She wouldn't let bones be scattered about. Nothing would put her springs in danger.

Jamie stepped forward, swinging the shovel at the fox's head. The shovel hit its skull with a sickening crack. The fox fell with a whimper, limbs shaking, blood leaking from his ears. Watching the fox take its dying breath, her heart heavy, she kneeled beside him. She hadn't meant to kill the poor thing. Only meant for him to drop the damn bone. She must have swung that shovel harder than she realized.

Now she'd have three bodies to bury instead of two.

A shadow moved inside the cave's entrance. Not the way a shadow would move from the rippling of water, more like it had tucked itself deeper into the cave.

Jamie stood. The water rippled with agitation, but only within the cave. What the hell? Something was in there. No way she'd risk going inside. She'd use the fox to figure out what was going on. It'd be a shame for it to die for nothing.

She grabbed the fox's tail and threw him in the water. Nothing too unusual about a dead fox, even if someone found him. Maybe whatever it was would still be hungry. If it was, and it was in the water as she suspected, it might like a fresh fox. That's what she was hoping. Jamie's joints reminded her that she'd missed her full morning soak, but she didn't dare get in the water until she figured out what might be in the cave.

First things first, the kid's would be stinking soon if she didn't get them buried.

It hadn't taken long for the flies to find their bodies. They swarmed every crevasse, depositing eggs and filth. In no time at all there'd be nothing but maggots and rot. Nature had a way of disposing of bodies efficiently.

She examined the mess before shaking out the tarp. The wound markings were strange. Almost smooth at the edges, but not entirely uniform.

They didn't look like knife wounds or anything a human might be capable of. They didn't look like animal bites, either.

The little flesh remaining reminded her of something that had been gnawed on by tiny, very sharp teeth. Like the pieces of cheese left in a mousetrap, only much smaller gnaw marks. Smaller than mice. Too small for anything she'd ever seen.

Thermophiles were the only things that'd survive the hot mineral water. Or maybe something in those weird stories that Aaron always went on about. Cryptic tales, she thought, he'd called them. She'd have to pay more attention.

She threw a tarp over the mess of goo and gore, wrapping both bodies to contain the smell. She'd only need to drag them a few meters into the dense forest, bury, and then cover them with forest litter. No one would ever find them. Unless they brought dogs, which they wouldn't without a vehicle. No vehicle, no way to tell just where the kids might have run off to.

Grabbing the edge of the tarp, Jamie yanked. It slid across the tall weeds with ease. Whatever had...eaten them? She didn't have a better explanation. Whatever had happened made them much lighter to handle. Had to be thankful for the small things.

Chapter Three

Those bodies had been gnawed on by something, but what? Whatever she'd seen inside the cave?

Jamie waited next to the water, pepper spray in one hand, buck knife in the other. The fox's tail floated on the surface like a furry fishing bobber. Half an hour had gone by, and she hadn't seen a thing. Watching the water within the cave, she found nothing but stillness.

Birds chirping in the forest choir. Sulfur wafting from the pool. Like any other peaceful morning in the woods, except there was nothing normal about it. She'd never seen anything like the damage done to those bodies.

What if whatever had done it was watching and waiting for her to leave?

The hair on the back of her neck pricked up. Nothing but the wind, that's all. The bushes rustled. She had to quit letting this situation get in her head.

There was probably a simple answer to what happened. Once she found out what it was, she'd relax and enjoy her soaks again. That's what she told herself, but it wasn't convincing, even to her.

She'd found an old hunting blind late last autumn not too far from the springs. If she'd been on her own, she would have cleared it immediately, but Aaron had con- vinced her to wait since the road was already impassable from the snowfall.

The blind was still there. Might be a good place to watch from, just in case whatever had done this was skittish.

Before leaving the fox near the shore of the pool, she tied a rope around its neck and the other end around a nearby boulder. She didn't want the fox dragged off.

She climbed the big tree that held the blind. It was sturdy enough, the tree and the blind. Whoever had made it knew what they were doing. Climbing the last rung, she found herself out of breath, body letting her know she wasn't in her twenties anymore. Still, not too bad for almost sixty.

She settled into the wooden seat resting on the branch. From there, she had a marvelous view of the springs, the

mountains and her cabin. Her cabin. That was unexpect-
ed. The way things were positioned didn't look accidental.
Damn fine view right through her bedroom window. Was
this motherfucker hunting animals or her? Pervert.

She'd met plenty of them in her life, more than she cared
to think about. It was one reason she'd gone into forestry,
to get away from the weirdoes.

She sat in the blind watching. The sun found its way
overhead, yet nothing had taken the bait. She waited as
long as possible without Aaron getting suspicious. Still
nothing.

Coming out of the tree, she jumped the last half-meter.
Reverberations from the impact ran up her legs, making
her hips and back scream. Recovering for a moment, she
assessed the springs, the fox, the late morning calm. Maybe
the thing was nocturnal?

She untied the rope. Dragging the sopping wet fox into
the brush, she decided she'd come back this evening. For
now, she needed to touch base with Aaron. Make sure he
kept himself good and busy on the other side of the rec
area.

When she got to the creek, Aaron was hard at work,
stacking rocks along the shoreline. A hoe and geo textile
material leaned against a giant fir.

"Looks like you're making progress. Want some help?" Jamie asked.

Aaron finished stacking the rocks for the section he was working on. "About done with the footer rocks. Then, only five rows to go." His dark blonde hair hung over one eye.

"Alright. Let's get to work." She grabbed the hoe.

They worked in silence for a good part of the afternoon. Aaron respected Jamie's preference for no distractions while she worked. The unspoken agreement was that once break-time rolled around, Jamie would listen to Aaron's stories. She didn't really mind. They were interesting sometimes.

Aaron sat on a boulder beside the creek, pulling off his waders.

"You know there's been cryptid sightings all over the park. Big foot is pretty common knowledge around here, so why not the rest? That's the question I've been asking."

"Well, what'd you come up with? I know you want to tell me." Jamie looked at him and smiled. It felt awkward on her face, she so rarely did it. It took a lot of work to look normal, and she didn't exhaust herself for just anyone. Plus, unlike Aaron, her teeth were much less than perfect. Her family couldn't afford the expensive dental work and braces that Aaron had so obviously had.

"Here's how I see it. People only believe what they want. Hairy humanoid? Sure. Shapeshifting bloodsucker? Suddenly, they're out. One is no more ridiculous than the other. Doesn't have to be magic either. Things in nature are known for changing shape and appearance, just look at chameleon's, tadpoles, and butterflies." He waited for her response.

"Well, Aaron. Those are mighty fine thoughts." Bloodsuckers? That was a new one. Maybe she'd find out more. "Bloodsuckers, huh?"

"Yeah, you know, vampires, chupacabras, wendigo, many names, but they all suck blood, eat flesh, whatever. There's a reason communion is the blood and body of Christ. Healers have used human blood and flesh since the beginning of time, but no one wants to talk about—"

Crashing and crunching from the bushes interrupted Aaron. He and Jamie looked towards the sound. Jamie put one hand on her knife and the other on a can of pepper spray, like a gunslinger in the Wild West. The pose was nearly innate. She'd had plenty of practice as a kid going ground hog plunking with her dad and hating every second of it.

As the leaves and branches rustled wildly, she waited to find out which would be the most appropriate weapon.

She took a few slow steps backwards, away from the danger.

A large brown nose poked through the huckleberries. Then its forehead and shoulders erupted from the bushes as it stood on hind legs.

She should have known. It was that time of year. The early season berries must have brought the bruin out of hibernation. Aaron slowly moved towards Jamie and away from where the bear stood, swinging its large head back and forth in curiosity and dominance.

The bear huffed. Jamie and Aaron were trained well enough to stay small and unthreatening.

Jamie had the pepper spray unholstered and ready. Unusual for a bear to attack, but better to be prepared than caught unaware. With the weird things going on around the park, who knew what might happen.

The bear grunted and dropped to all fours. Whipping its head over one shoulder, it bounded into the forest, apparently deciding that two humans were too much trouble.

"That's the closest I've been. Way to get the adrenaline flowing," Aaron said, his hand coming out of his pocket in a grip that was familiar to Jamie.

She had seen bears and a gun grip many times, but unlike the bears, guns weren't allowed in the park, not even for a warden. She didn't know much about Aaron. He never talked about family or friends or where he came from. The only personal things she knew were from his resume.

He'd graduated from a university in Europe she'd never heard of, but he didn't have an accent that she noticed. This was his third post since graduating. Most of his previous experience had been in visitor centers, which surprised Jamie, seeing as the kid was shyer than her.

"If that didn't fill your drawers, let me grab you a soda. I've got a fresh delivery at the cabin." Jamie hopped on her bike. "Be right back. Unless you need to go change your shorts?"

Aaron laughed, staring into the brush. "You think it's gone?"

"That old bear isn't interested in us. Besides, I thought you were the big bad sasquatch hunter?" Jamie yelled over her shoulder as she rode away.

The sun dropped behind the mountains as Jamie sat in the blind, waiting. Too dark to see with the naked eye, but the infrared binoculars kept her vision clear.

A ripple in the springs caught her attention. Waves rolled across the surface of the water as if the wind had picked up. Only there wasn't any wind. She'd have certainly felt it on her perch. The tree leaves and limbs were perfectly still.

Then, the fox's tail dunked beneath the water. Once. Twice. Three times.

All she saw was that roiling water. Then, the whole damn fox bobbed below the surface. When it returned, its flesh hung in tattered shreds. The water grew alive with movement and chunks of fox flesh. She couldn't understand or believe what she was seeing.

Then, the springs went completely still, nothing moved except the remnants of the fox gently floating on the surface, bits of skin and meat hanging from white bones, like a papier mâché piñata beaten and ripped apart to access the treats hidden within.

Jamie dropped from the tree, hitting the ground with a thud.

As she walked towards the fox, a small ripple caught her attention. A few centimeters from where the fox's nose used to be, there was something moving, fluffy and green.

It dunked beneath the water, stirring of its own accord. A sentient blob of algae, blue-green and fuzzy like her pet bunny when she was a kid. Well, her bunny had been white, but just as fluffy. She hadn't thought about Fuzzy in a long time.

On the farm Jamie grew up on, animals were commodities, products, not pets. When Fuzzy didn't reproduce the way bunnies are known for, she was slated for the dinner table by Jamie's father. Jamie had fallen in love with the bunny. She spent all her time between chores, petting and talking to her. No way was she going to let Dad kill her, so she hid her in the field and snuck food to her. She kept her like that for a few months. Then, winter hit and snowed them in for a week. By the time Jamie got back to her, she'd frozen to death.

Jamie had barely glimpsed the water creature before it was gone. Fuzzy. That's what she'd call it, because everything needed a name. She watched a while longer, hoping to see it again. The water's glass-like surface broken only by a few bubbles gurgling up from the cracks.

It must be her imagination, but every time she drew near the springs, her stomach growled with emptiness and her mind filled with hot rage. How dare anyone disrespect her springs. Her emotions had always been muted shades, the fairest of pastels. Now they were bright, sharp colors like fuchsia and emerald.

Pulling the rope, she dragged the fox, pieces of ragged flesh scraped onto the jagged rocks at the shoreline. They glistened like pork belly ripe for the eating, Jamie stopped herself from grabbing one.

The wildlife would eat well tonight.

At least she wouldn't have to bury the fox. He'd be gone by morning. Nothing unusual about a mostly eaten wild animal in the forest, even if someone happened to find it. Some danger of drawing predators, but she'd happily risk that. Maybe she'd catch one of Aaron's sasquatches. She didn't really believe in such nonsense, but she didn't know how to explain Fuzzy either.

There were no obvious teeth marks on the fox. Only more gnaw-like marks, dull and ragged, just like the kids. Fuzzy must have a hell of an appetite. She'd never heard or seen anything about carnivorous algae. Although blue-green algae was one of the few things that lived within the water. It didn't swim or eat animals. Nothing about this made any sense at all.

She'd have to be ready if she wanted to catch it. It would be looking to feed again. She was sure of that.

A pet from her holy springs. Her skin tingled with the thought.

Chapter Four

The next day, after having lunch with Aaron and helping him shore up the creek, Jamie went back to her cabin to fashion a trap for Fuzzy. It was endangering her beloved springs and keeping her from enjoying her waters. Her body ached.

Knowing Fuzzy was somewhere around, even if it only fed at night, creeped her out. And she wasn't too sure it only fed at night. Over the winter months small corpses, birds, squirrels, and a rabbit, had floated away from the cave opening. Fuzzy had likely been the culprit all along.

A carnivorous fluffy mass of blue-green algae that moved of its own accord. She had to be careful, there was much more to learn. She didn't want to hurt it. She'd set up an aquarium and feed Fuzzy rats. Plenty of them around in the springtime.

The rats. She'd use them as bait. Netting, or cheesecloth maybe? Cheesecloth might be the only thing with a fine enough mesh, but she wasn't sure how she'd get it around Fuzzy.

While she rifled around in the shed, Aaron walked up the driveway, that smug looking sheriff attached to his hip. She likely wouldn't even have seen them until they were in her face, except for the sound of that sheriff spitting his chew in her woods. No mistaking that.

Didn't look like that old codger of a sheriff was giving up, which was mighty unfortunate for both of them. Jamie stepped through the doorway, brushing dust off her gloves. "Hey, sheriff. What brings you back out here? Hope you found those kids."

The sheriff narrowed his eyes.

"That's the thing. We found tire tracks coming in, but none leaving. Nothing. Sure looks like someone was here and didn't leave." He rubbed his two-day stubbled chin. "You wouldn't happen to know where else we might look? Might just need to bring in a search party. It'd cost a bunch of money. The boy's parents are important people in town and have some pull with the mayor."

"Don't know what those kids might have gotten themselves into, but I do know this is a tough area to search. Between the terrain and wildlife, rescue efforts rarely find anyone if they've truly gone missing." She gave the sheriff her friendliest smile. She didn't need any trouble with him today. "Probably just a couple of love-struck kids. They'll be making their way home sooner or later."

"Hmm, maybe." The sheriff fiddled with his shirt collar. "Aaron mentioned kids like to come here and party? Sometimes poachers too?"

Aaron shifted uncomfortably, looking at the ground. Now it was Jamie's turn to narrow her eyes. He knew she didn't like him talking to the sheriff. When Aaron looked up, he wore a whooped puppy face. Jamie avoided his eyes.

"We find blinds and party spots around here now and then. I surely don't remember where, amongst all these trees." She swept her hand around, gesturing to the forest in every direction.

Jamie knew nearly every foot of this area, but the sheriff didn't need to know that. Other than the blind, there hadn't been much action since things had closed, better to keep the sheriff busy with something though. The last party Jamie broke up, had been a few years back. It'd led to a handful of gates being added to the roads after a couple kids ran off and got lost in the woods for an afternoon.

Luckily, they hadn't gone far before Jamie found them. Nowadays kids weren't as interested in the woods.

"Of course. Yeah, I don't expect you to remember an exact tree or nothing like that. Just a general area. I don't want to call a search party."

The last sounded like a threat to Jamie.

Aaron shifted his gaze back to the ground. Something off with him. Had he seen something? Might be a good idea for Jamie to find out, but not with the sheriff here.

"Could you grab the rat traps from the shed, Aaron? Noticed tracks in the cabin. Damn things come in every spring." She smiled, nodding her head towards the shed door.

"Sure thing." Aaron stepped inside the shed.

"Just drop em off at the cabin and you can take the rest the day off. Go hiking or something," Jamie shouted.

Aaron was always itching to go hiking. It'd be better if he wasn't around for a bit. Jamie sidled next to the sheriff, nodding her head towards where he'd come from. "Let's walk down to the parking lot. I'll show you where I found the beer cans."

"If you see any signs of those kids or remember anything, let me know, Aaron." The sheriff yelled towards the shed, never taking his eyes off Jamie.

As she and the sheriff walked back to the parking lot, she had a hard time keeping her mind off the springs.

"Wish I could help more, but like I said, there's been so many spots. Lots of times, they never use the same place more than once. Pick any old area and there's probably been a blind or a party there at one time or another. The fines have done a pretty good job of discouraging that sort of thing in the last few years." Jamie tried to look dutifully sad. "Maybe just two or three a year anymore." Jamie stopped and pointed at the ditch next to the parking lot. "Couple cans and a couple butts, I already disposed of them."

Nothing but rocks and a few struggling wildflowers in the ditch.

"I'll keep looking. You don't mind, do you?" Sheriff Anders tipped his hat and headed on up the service road without waiting for an answer.

The last thing she needed was that goddammed sheriff poking around. She strode up beside him.

"Tell you what, I'll walk you to all the spots I can think of, at least the ones that have been used recently."

"Lead the way, Jamie." The sheriff winked.

She hated when he winked at her. Nothing friendly in it at all. The sooner she rid herself of him, the better.

After an hour of pointing out random trees and meadows, the Sheriff finally gave up and went home. Their walk didn't turn up anything interesting. At least, as far as the sheriff knew. Jamie, on the other hand, had developed a plan while trying not to listen to the sheriff's inane musings.

Now, she just had to catch a rat.

CHAPTER FIVE

Missy drove slowly up the mountain, watching for remnants of the old logging road they were told about by the guy at the gas station. Leon and Dwayne chatted in the backseat, as Rita, sitting shotgun, passed the joint to Leon.

Missy turned hard left into the long-overgrown weeds. The VW's lift cleared all but the tallest vegetation, plowing down the dilapidated road.

"Wahoo! That's the way!" Leon's ass lifted off the seat as they cruised towards where they'd heard they'd find the hot springs. "Man, don't make me drop the joint."

Rita and Missy laughed as they all bounced along.

"You better hand it over before you lose it," Rita said, reaching back between the seats.

Missy hit the brakes, lurching them all forward.

"What the hell, Missy?" Dwayne said, holding his neck.

"Almost there. It'll be a short walk. Bug's not going any farther," Missy said.

"Guy said to watch for wardens. Guess they've been patrolling pretty heavy," Dwayne said.

"Who the fuck they think they are, shutting down nature? Man, fuck that." Leon got out, slamming the car door.

The others piled out.

"I don't see any water. Nothing but forest out here," Leon said.

Rita pointed into the tree line.

"You see that mist rising?" She winked, crinkling the small green heart on her upper cheek.

Sure enough, there was a billowing cloud of steam rolling between the evergreens. Late afternoon sun filtered by partial clouds gave the forest a mystical feel. It had taken longer than they'd thought to get there, and they were antsy to get a bath.

Rita didn't waste time. disappearing into the trees towards the steam. Leon wasn't far behind. Hot and sweaty from traveling across the country with all their belongings. They'd worked their way up from California, stopping at every hot springs they'd found in the tattered guidebook Missy carried.

Dwayne leaned against the VW.

"Doesn't feel right," he said, glancing around.

"Aw, come on. We haven't seen a single person, let alone a warden. Probably off for the day," Missy said, eyes pleading.

"Let's do this. Not too long though?" Dwayne said.

"Agreed." Missy grabbed his hand, pulling him until he matched step with her seconds later.

They joined Leon, cutting through the bushes towards the steam. Lifting a branch and ducking beneath, they emerged. The grotto opened ahead. Rita stood at the edge of the pool, yanking off her pants.

"Last one in's a rotten egg." She jumped in, splashing up to her knees at the water's edge. They all laughed, taking off their clothes. Rita waded deeper.

"Damn, these needed a washing." She rubbed her panties between her hands, letting the water carry away the crusties.

Missy pranced into the pool, bare assed.

"Ah, it feels so good." She dunked her hair, scrubbing her scalp. Her face peeking through the surface as she rinsed.

Leon walked through the water towards the cave.

"This is awesome!" He poked his head inside.

"Dude, you never know what might hide in there." Dwayne shook his head, his long grey beard swaying. "I've seen some crazy shit."

Leon laughed.

"Let's find out." He stepped inside.

Rita bounded towards the cavernous opening, plodding through the waist deep water. Missy lifted her head, watching as Rita went inside.

"Kids'll be kids." Dwayne shrugged.

Leon and Rita were certainly not kids, but Missy supposed compared to her and Dwayne, they were close enough.

"Doesn't look safe." Missy shook her head.

"Let'm have their fun." Dwayne took a quick dip and went back to shore.

Missy grabbed her clothes and dunked them in the water.

Giggles wafted from the cave. Then, guttural noises. Leon and Rita messing around again. Dwayne laughed, sitting his butt on a rock beside the pool and lighting a fatty.

Movement at the edge of the forest caught Missy's attention. No sooner did she look than the thing, a blur of black and gray membranous skin, landed atop Dwayne.

She couldn't understand what she was seeing. Dwayne fought with something that looked like a translucent gray tarp as they fell and rolled on the ground.

Rips, tears, and screaming drowned out the birdsong.

Dwayne's hair went bright red, blood running down his face. As Missy tried to make sense of what she saw, the thing's claws scalped Dwayne, exposing bone and bubbly brains.

Missy screamed and ran toward the cave for protection. Slow motion through the waist deep water, she'd almost made it to the opening. Rita and Leon's screams joined the wet sloppy sounds coming from the thing and what was left of Dwayne.

Missy turned. Rita fell out of the cave, body covered in wounds as though someone had tried to skin her but missed a few spots. She lurched towards Missy, grabbing her shoulders. Missy went under. Bubbles surrounded her as Rita's weight came down on her. Missy struggled to get away, paddling backwards. In a whoosh, Rita disappeared into the darkness beyond the cave's entrance.

Missy dove for the side of the pool, getting onto the bank in seconds. The forest had gone silent. She ran over dirt, rocks, and sticks. No time to worry about any of that now. She'd almost reached the tree line on her way to the safety of the VW when a thud sounded directly behind her. She looked over her shoulder.

There it stood, nearly eight feet tall, leathery skin with membranous tissue between its long arms and body. Webbed fingers ending in long talons, like a nightmare flying squirrel combined with Aquaman. Its face might have been human except for the grotesque skin and teeth. As it opened its mouth, the fangs hung past its narrow chin.

Thick mucus dripped down her neck as the creature's fangs sunk into her flesh.

Chapter Six

Jamie went to the springs that evening with her supplies, including a live trap with a rat inside. Maybe live bait would bring Fuzzy into the light. She had to make sure she was right about its need for darkness. If not, she'd wait for nightfall.

She tied a life vest to the trap and placed it, rat and all, into the water. She hoped this would bring it out, where she could get a better look and plan its capture. She waited behind the bushes for Fuzzy or nightfall, whichever appeared first.

She jerked her head up, opening her eyes. It took a moment to remember where she was. Surrounded by darkness, and annoyed with herself for falling asleep, she lifted the binoculars. The pool bubbled and roiled. The trap bobbed beneath the surface.

In the few short steps it took to get to the water, Fuzzy had eaten everything but the metal trap and the rat's bones. A faint green ripple entered the cave. She'd need something larger than a rat to keep Fuzzy eating longer. A nice fatty would be more buoyant too. Help her get a better look.

The sheriff. Big old gut of his would make an excellent bobber. She added an apple in his mouth while he floated in the pool of her mind and got a real good laugh. Hurt her sides, laughing so much. She'd never do a thing like that in real life, but boy did it feel nice to imagine. One way or another, she needed to catch Fuzzy.

"What are you doing, Jamie?" Aaron startled her, standing not more than a few meters away.

She hadn't noticed him walk up the trail. Where had her mind been?

"Aaron! I'm glad you're here," she said, using her excited voice, but not so much as to make him suspicious. "I think I've found one of your cryptic creatures."

She'd use his love of legends to her advantage. He'd never call the authorities on his favorite pastime, the cryptics.

"Cryptid," Aaron corrected. "Here, where?"

"Well, I'm not sure, but something is living in the cave. And I've never seen anything like it." Jamie lifted the trap, rattling the bones. "Whatever it was that got through this." She pointed at the wire mesh. "And did this." She rattled the bones again. "We can't let the sheriff find out or he'll surely kill it."

Aaron's grin spread across his face in what Jamie thought might be the first expression of joy she'd ever seen on him.

"I want you to help me catch it," she said.

Aaron raised one manicured eyebrow.

"There's something in the cave and it has been eating animals. I still haven't gotten a good look at it, but this is what it does." Jamie rattled the bones in the cage again. No way was she mentioning the kids, and she didn't.

Aaron held out his hand. She let him take the trap. Turning it every which way, he examined the contents.

"That really is something. Nothing but bones." Aaron twirled the trap with a low whistle. "I've never seen anything like it."

"Got me thinking about your cryptics, uh, cryptids. Bloodsuckers, flesh eaters, and the like. Surely don't know anything in nature that would do this." Jamie waited for Aaron's response.

"That is strange." Aaron kept looking inside the trap, as if waiting for something more to appear.

He poked his finger inside and touched the skull. It rolled away from the spine. Hollow.

"Ate the organs and all. Fascinating."

Jamie reached for the trap, and Aaron let her take it.

"Let's catch it. I've got some ideas."

Aaron grinned, and Jamie smiled, showing her crooked front teeth.

They put another rat in the water. No trap. Knocked it out with some bear sedative. It didn't take much.

"There it is," Aaron whispered.

Jamie had almost dozed off. When she lifted the night vision goggles, the water was alive with motion. A dark green shape moved toward the rat. The rat was pulled from its spot along the shore into deeper water.

It bobbed and disappeared.

Aaron ran to the springs, but Fuzzy had already retreated into the cave. It was fast.

"You weren't kidding. It's amazing. What all have you tried feeding it?" Aaron asked.

"Feeding it? I've been trying to trap it, not feed it."

"Yeah, well, what have you used in the trap? What animals? Have you tried store meat?"

"Aaron, I just need to get it out of the springs." Jamie already regretted telling Aaron about Fuzzy.

She didn't want to share it or the healing waters, not even with him.

"Yeah, yeah, we will. This is all going to help. Seeing it out here in the wild is really something." Aaron positively glowed.

Jamie wasn't sure where else they might see one, other than in the wild. Didn't look like any zoo animal she'd ever seen. Soon it would be her pet though. What if Aaron didn't want her to keep it?

"Let's get on with capturing it. Last thing we need is that sheriff finding out." Jamie already grew tired of Aaron's excitement.

This wasn't the Aaron cryptid catcher show.

The only thing that mattered was protecting the springs. If that meant playing along with Aaron, so be it.

Chapter Seven

J amie and Aaron left the bones in the water. It wasn't unknown for animals to come to the springs to die. Nothing strange about finding remains, especially ones that were picked clean.

They'd tried feeding Fuzzy thawed out burger, but no interest. They'd even tried roadkill, thanks to a daredevil squirrel running in front of Jamie's truck. Day old dead squirrel didn't tempt Fuzzy either. Then the crows found the squirrel, and that was the end of that. Previously killed animals were okay, but not so long dead that the blood wasn't fresh. If the blood had congealed, Fuzzy didn't want it.

In Jamie's opinion none of this mattered. As far as she was concerned, Aaron polluted her springs and hindered catching Fuzzy, for no good reason. Jamie had discovered live bait was Fuzzy's favorite long before Aaron's involvement. What did any of the rest of it matter?

Then, Aaron convinced her to experiment with size. How big of an animal would Fuzzy consume? Turned out there were limits to Fuzzy's hunger. They'd made it to yearling deer before bits of flesh were left tattered on the bones again.

As the days went on, Jamie enjoyed feeding Fuzzy. Each successive feeding, its mass grew a smidge, and it required more to satisfy it. None of this got her any closer to getting back in the water or catching Fuzzy. She was tempted to just soak and see what happened.

"We can't keep doing this. We need to catch it," Jamie said.

Her joints ached, and her skin itched like crazy. She tried not to scratch. She hadn't had an arthritis flare this bad since she'd taken the post here.

"Any suggestions?" Aaron asked as he crouched next to her, pulling another empty rope in to shore.

"You're the great sasquatch hunter. Shouldn't you be able to catch a fuzzy blob?" Jamie asked.

Aaron smiled.

"Maybe...maybe I do have an idea. Floating the bait didn't work. What about sinking? What if we weigh it down? Once they feed, we throw a fine mesh net over the top. Then, we drag it along the bottom, not too far because we'll set it up at the edge and the algae monster won't be able to take off with the bait because of the added weight."

"How are we going to weigh down the bait? And how the hell are we going to pull the thing once we've made it so heavy?" Jamie asked.

None of this sounded good to her. Aaron tapped his forehead.

"Let me think. I'm going to work this out." He gave her his gentle face.

It was the one that reminded her most of Jonny. Of the last look she'd seen before that tractor's plow blades went into him. Not fear, not pain, just a real gentle look, like he forgave her. Her father never had. He reminded her every chance he got until his death. As if her own guilt wasn't punishment enough. She hadn't known that Jonny had camped in the field that night.

It was daybreak when Jamie awoke to plow Daddy's field. She'd stayed up late reading a story about a woman traveling the Canadian back country on horseback in the most recent National Geographic, and her vision was blurred. The kitchen sink held a few dirty dishes she'd take care of later. She opened the fridge. A couple eggs, small block of cheese, and some butter. Dad would want those.

In the cupboard, a couple slices of bread and a bit of jam were all that was left. She'd leave that for Jonny.

Grabbing a quick cup of coffee from the pot she'd made the day before, she swallowed it down cold. Dad lay sprawled across the living room floor, empty Gibson's bottle beside him. Their hand-me-down couch and chair threadbare and sunken. Black-and-white TV playing static. Jamie crossed the room to turn it off.

Dad grabbed her ankle.

"You better have breakfast ready by nine," he mumbled.

"Sure thing, Daddy." The field was small, and she figured she'd have it done in a couple hours, plenty of time to make his breakfast.

"Don't break anything before I get up." He rolled over and went back to sleep.

Fourteen-years-old and head of the household since Mom died, Jamie did her best to keep up with her chores, but never to her father's satisfaction. She'd surprise him with a freshly plowed field. She'd helped lots of times, but today she'd do it on her own.

The safflower had finished blooming. All the small yellow flowers had been harvested for seeds. The remaining greens, she'd plow into the soil for mulch. She always watched carefully for the movement of rodents and such. Some were unavoidable, but she tried her best.

She'd plowed three rows without a hitch. Then, a strange shape in front of her blades caught her attention. Jonny in his army green sleeping bag didn't budge until it was much too late. His eyes opened wide. Then, that gentle expression.

A short scream and blood splattered across Jamie and the tractor's fender. By the time she reacted to stop the tractor, pieces of Jonny were churned into the soil, painting the field in his bodily fluids. She hopped down. Her feet sinking into the freshly tilled earth, she ran piece to piece, gathering Jonny into her arms. Holding as much as possible, tears streaming, she ran towards their little white farmhouse, trying her best to hold onto Jonny. Parts of him slipped from her hands and arms leaving a trail of Jonny behind.

She ran up the steps two at a time, arms slippery with blood, bile, and feces. A glob of intestines uncoiled and hung underfoot. She tripped as she reached the last step, falling face first onto the porch intermingled with her mutilated brother. The stench was horrific.

That's where her father had found her, splayed on the porch, bawling, pieces of Jonny scattered around and beneath her, covered in blood, mucus, and feces. He turned and went back inside, leaving her to clean up and call the authorities.

It had been so long ago, yet the slip of his goo and stench of his waste never left, like she'd tucked a piece of Jonny away and carried it to this very day.

"Yeah, okay J—" Jamie stopped herself before saying her dead brother's name. "Uh, Aaron."

The glimmer in Aaron's eyes told her he had a plan, but she wasn't sure she trusted him. More and more it occurred to her that he played games with her, doing little more than stalling Fuzzy's capture. Her body needed the water sooner rather than later. It grew stiffer and more painful by the day.

Took her almost an hour to get out of bed that morning. She didn't want to imagine what tomorrow morning would bring. The only thing that gave her relief was sleep, and that was restless and sporadic.

Jamie rose early the next morning with about three hours of sleep. Her hips and back ached, stabbing pains seared them with every movement. Slowly she maneuvered to the edge of the bed and swung her legs over the side. Pushing up with her arms, her wrists and elbows crunched and burned. All the ditches dug, outbuildings built, and miles traveled hadn't prepared her for this.

She sat on the edge of the bed, testing the floor with her toes, then her feet. Her ankles shrieked and her knees almost buckled. She couldn't resist the call of her water. The silky smoothness. The layer of soft protection from the minerals. The warmth. The colors. Oh, she longed for the colors. Everything had been grey lately, not pastel, just dingy grey.

There'd been no sign that Fuzzy would come out in the daylight. She'd tried everything to coax it out. As long as she stayed away from the cave, everything would be fine, better than fine. Maybe she'd feel human again—as if she ever really had. Her joints cracked and popped. Hot and inflamed from the neck down, if she didn't get in the water, she'd die. She counted her pain pills. there were enough to go to sleep for good. Might as well risk the healing springs first.

The thought helped her walk to the kitchen. She made a pot of coffee. Her muscles and joints awoke, limbering ever so slightly, bit by bit.

Still dark, her front porch offered a view of the sunrise in the east. Sipping her coffee from her deadwood chair, she waited. As soon as the sun rose, she pedaled to the springs for her morning soak.

The fluid motion of pedaling helped her knees and ankles relax, but her wrists and back made her thankful for the short ride. The grotto shined like a mirage or something straight out of a fairy tale. Birds sang and two squirrels chased each other around the nearest tree. Jamie stacked her jacket, shirt, and pants on the bike rack. Then, slipped out of her boots. She carried a small towel to dry off and placed it on a rock by the shore.

Wearing only her underwear and sports bra, she stepped into the pool. The water wrapped her differently. Almost alive, as if stroking her. Millions of tiny fingers washing away the pain. Her body relaxed, melting into the water. The heat in her joints dissipated, bringing comforting warmth. Where her skin ended and the water began, now a mystery. Her breathing slowed and she tipped her head back closing her eyes.

Magenta and burgundy lit her mind with rage and hunger, bright and alive. How long had she starved herself? How long had she denied herself justified revenge? People and food flashed through her thoughts, until becoming one and the same. She dove beneath the water.

The world softened to fluid warmth, insulating her from all but the swirl of beautiful vibrant colors. A low hum, murmuring, not voices but emotions. Of hunger and desire, but also comfort and love. A collective contentment embracing infinity.

She gasped and drew in water. Surfacing, she gagged and coughed. Water expelled from her lungs. Standing waist deep near the entrance to the cave, bright yellow fear overwhelmed her. A piece of something stuck to her arm. Fleshy, almost the size of a loonie, with a small green heart tattoo.

She flicked it into the water and fled the springs, but not before receiving Fuzzy's call.

Chapter Eight

J amie's phone rang as she drove into town for supplies. Local dispatcher, Mandy, was on the other end. Mandy was always professional at first, but loved to dish gossip once business was out of the way.

"Jamie, wanted to let you know the sheriff won't be coming by today. Guess those kids' parents decided they ran off after all."

Relieved to hear it, Jamie figured running off was a more comforting story to their parents than the alternative. Definitely better than knowing the truth. A flash of the kids' bodies floated through her mind. The tatters of flesh now rainbow colors. Horrible, yet she felt more alive than she had in decades.

Mandy continued without Jamie saying a word.

"Parents decided to wait for them to get tired and come home. Hoping they're right, because the rumor around town is that boy might have kidnapped the girl. You know, her family is new in town. No one wants to accuse the star hockey player or go up against his powerful father."

Good news for Jamie. A bit of guilt tugged at her chest.

"Thanks for letting me know. I'm headed into town. Want me to bring you anything?" Jamie hated gossip, but it was best to have Mandy on her side.

Plus, Jamie needed to keep track of any suspicions. Mandy knew everyone in town. Funny how much someone else's opinion made a difference in how others treated you. Jamie learned a few things over the years about people, and that was one of them. Better to have friends than enemies.

"I have been hankering for an ice cream from Old Joes. Would you mind?" Mandy asked.

"Done. I'll see you in a bit." Jamie hung up the phone.

A visit with Mandy hadn't been on her schedule today, but she'd keep it quick. Lots of work to be done in springtime around the park.

She pulled into the Quick Stop lot and shut off her truck. It took her a minute to steel herself for small talk. She hated chit-chat, almost as much as gossip, but had learned to play the game. The faster it was over, the better.

She laid her items on the counter. Pack of gum. Canadian Wildlife magazine. Five-pound package of beef.

Ralph stood behind the register. He was a stout, balding man that had worked there since his teens. Not much changed in these little towns over the years.

"How are things at the park?" Ralph asked.

"Preparing for the spring thaw. Got us a creek to shore up and some downed trees to clear. How's the family?"

"Timmy went and got himself married. Can't hardly believe it. Seems like yesterday he was just a kid. Still a kid to me, but now he might have some of his own. Can you imagine that? Me, a grandpa?"

Jamie could imagine, but Ralph didn't want to hear that.

"You're not old enough to be a grandpa. You tell that kid to slow down."

They both got a good laugh out of that. Jamie scooped her items off the counter.

"Congrats to all of you. Give them my best." She waved as she pushed the door open with her shoulder.

"Will do!" Ralph smiled, showing the gaps where his missing molars once lived.

One more stop, two counting the delivery of Mandy's ice cream, and she'd get back to her mountain. She hated every moment of being away.

Luckily, Old Joe's had a drive-thru so at least she didn't have to go inside.

"Double scoop of chocolate," she told the ordering screen.

As she pulled forward, a boy, about twelve, Jonny's age when he'd died, walked out of the ice cream shop. He was so intent on his bubble gum sugar cone that he didn't even look as he approached the road. Jamie shouted. The boy turned as a car whizzed by less than an arm's length away.

"Careful, you almost got hit!" Jamie shouted from her truck.

The kid flipped her off. Then, he looked both ways before crossing the road. Little brat. She should have let the car splatter him. The cashier handed her Mandy's ice cream cone in exchange for payment, and she pulled away, flipping the kid off as she drove by. One last stop.

Jamie parked at the sheriff's office and got out of the truck. Upon entering the building, Jamie waved to Mandy and Sheriff Ann Lewis. Sheriff Ann generally stayed in town. Afraid of bears, from what Jamie had heard.

Mandy clapped her hands, vibrating in her chair behind the front desk. Big hair and lots of makeup, she did all the emergency dispatching for the area.

"You are such a doll! Thank you, honey!"

Jamie hated these endearments, but she tried to smile without looking like she was grimacing. She handed Mandy her cone.

"Of course. I'd love to chat, but lots of work on the mountain." Jamie backed towards the door.

"Oh, wait just a second, honey. I've got something for you." Mandy opened her desk drawer and pulled out a sparkling gold star. "I bought a dozen. We all get to be a star." She pointed to the one on her sweater.

A big tacky looking pin, but Jamie took it to keep the peace. She gave Mandy a closed lip smile and nodded. Sheriff Ann waved from her corner desk as Jamie walked out.

On the way up the mountain road, she rolled down her window, breathing the crisp spring air. Early season wildflowers bloomed with fragrance, mixing with heavy pine and forest mulch. Her heart and breathing slowed. A natural smile played on her lips.

She hardly believed her eyes when she saw the Volkswagen. The wildflowers and grasses growing on the long-forgotten forest road hadn't sprung back enough to hide the faded yellow bug, jacked up for off roading. It couldn't have been there long. More kids looking for fun and mischief. No sign of whoever had been in it. There were no hiking trails nearby. Goddammit, they'd gone to the pool.

She cursed her luck. Suspicions were just dying down. The last thing she needed were more missing kids.

She hiked to the springs as quick as her legs would carry her. A few birds bathed along the shore, but the pool was otherwise empty. She eyed the opening to the cave. The bodies might still be in there, but she didn't have time to worry about that. She needed to get rid of the bug and whoever the hell owned it.

The distinctive sound of bike tires on gravel alerted her that Aaron pedaled up the road. He already knew about Fuzzy, but she didn't need him knowing they ate humans—and damn, what if it had eaten more than the two? She didn't think he'd be okay with that.

She walked down the trail toward him. The glare off his mountain bike shown in the distance. Trying to figure out what to say, she kicked a few rocks off the road.

Aaron pulled up beside her. Something about him seemed off. His hair was disheveled from the ride, but it was more than that. His eyes were shifty. She wasn't sure she trusted the kid anymore.

"Gorgeous afternoon. Any new bait?" Aaron asked.

He needed to leave. Jamie didn't think he'd seen the VW. She had to play it cautious if Fuzzy had indeed eaten these ones too. She had to make sure the evidence was gone before he found out more than she liked. She'd give him an errand or two.

"I've got a few things to do in the cabin. You finish the creek. Shouldn't take long. When you're done, go enjoy the sun." She lifted her eyes towards the sky.

That should get rid of him long enough for her to figure things out.

"I've got an idea for a new trap," Aaron said.

"Okay, yeah. Let's do it tomorrow, okay? We both deserve a bit of a break. The weather report says to expect rain in a few days. We need the creek finished." Jamie sighed.

"Gotta love spring rain." Aaron still straddled his bike.

"Come on, let's get it done and enjoy the day." She gave him a pat on the back.

Aaron waved as he rode off.

Jamie examined the water, looking for signs of the Volkswagen's occupants. So many leaves, bug carcasses and unidentified globules floated in suspension within the water. Impossible to tell, but a few were suspicious. Then, she remembered the tattooed heart. Whoever they were, it was much too late. She hadn't found any clothes to search for keys, so she'd need tools to hotwire the car. Whoever had come in that bug was surely dead by now. Fuzzy told her that much. The walk to her cabin was pleasant, she felt thirty again, maybe even twenty-five.

She sat on her couch. Her heart hadn't fully recovered from the panic of Aaron coming up that road. Putting her feet up and lying back, she rested her eyes. What if Aaron had seen the VW? No end of trouble it'd cause. She took a long, slow breath. She needed to rest, but first she'd have to deal with the bug

She awoke in a cold sweat, shirt drenched, the sun only an hour from sinking behind Three Sisters. Dammit, she hadn't meant to sleep the day away. She threw on her parka and boots and headed out the door.

When she got to the springs, Aaron's bike lay on the ground. No sign of him, anywhere. Did he go for a hike? If he did, he should've been back by now. Besides, there were no hiking trails near the springs, at least none that he'd be interested in. A short, overgrown, nature trail led from the upper parking lot around the springs, but that was about it. Dammit, where did he get off to? No unusual sounds, which told her he wasn't anywhere around here. Unless he'd gone in the cave? Jamie wasn't sure if that idea relieved or worried her. Had Fuzzy called him too? No, Fuzzy chose her.

No time for worrying, that VW needed to be taken care of. When she got to the place where she'd seen it earlier, the VW was gone. Near dark now, it was an enormous risk going into the springs, but she had to. What if the VW kids had hurt Fuzzy? What if Aaron was in there?

Aaron should have known better, but there was only one way to find out if anyone or their remains were still in the cave. She'd stay out of the cave, but maybe she could peek inside. If she saw anything close, she'd fish it out. She'd bring her fetching stick with her.

As Jamie drew closer to the water, a ripple rolled across the surface. She took off her boots and slowly dunked her toes in the springs. She waited. Nothing. No ripples. She must have imagined it.

Leaving her warden's uniform crumpled on the shoreline, she entered the water.

The silky softness enveloped her skin, soothed her itch, and lit every cell in her body with a swirling spectrum of blues, greens, and purples. Ecstasy. The way it caressed every part of her was delicious. She felt them, not it, definitely them, whatever they were. Their essence was a multitude of warmth and comfort, like being nestled in her mom's bosom. A memory she had forgotten until now. The soft, soothing love of a mother's hug. She wanted to feel that forever.

A scent, sweet like honey, rose from the pool. The water slicker and thicker, the consistency of oil. Energized and pain free, she wanted to remain here with them forever. A song, melodious and lovely, flitted from the cave. Familiar notes caught on the breeze. She peered inside and stepped forward. Something bobbed in the water ahead, beckoning.

A voice, gravelly and rasping, unmistakably the sheriff pulled her back to reality, and she popped outside the cave. The sheriff stood on the shore, a wad of chew in his lower lip, hands on hips.

"What are you doing in there, Jamie?"

She shielded her eyes from the flashlight he carried. Somehow, it had grown full dark in the few seconds she'd entered the cave.

"Mind giving me some privacy, sheriff? Thought I saw something, is all." Fresh bait stood before her, so close she smelled his pungent odor.

She laughed at these strange and morbid thoughts. The sheriff turned away.

"Give me a minute. Kind of embarrassing getting caught in my skivvies like this." Sliding out of the water, she grabbed her shirt and dried off. Then she pulled on the rest of her clothes. She thumbed the buck knife in her jacket pocket.

"Just a minute, sheriff." She'd left her boots off.

He'd never hear, never know, until it was too late. She smiled with new purpose. Feeding, the only thing that mattered.

She approached the sheriff from behind, grasping the handle of her knife. He must have sensed her movement because he turned towards her. Eyes wide as the knife slashed at him. He put up a hand. His hat fell as she plunged the knife into his neck.

He shouted, tobacco dribbling from his lip. He tried to lunge away. She twisted and pushed with all her might. The cartilage crunching and ripping. Blood spurted from the wound, spraying the sleeve of her jacket and across her face. Nothing a cold rinse of water wouldn't take care of. She licked the blood from her lips.

The sheriff whimpered as he crumpled to the ground. She pulled the knife from his neck, walked to the edge of the springs, and rinsed the blade. Full dark now, the water rippled with motion.

They were so hungry.

Chapter Nine

What they were, she still didn't know, but she wanted to care for them, merge with them, be surrounded by them. Every sacrifice would be worth it in the end.

Fishing the keys out of the sheriff's pocket and putting them in her own, she amazed herself with the icy blue calm running through her veins. Bear hugging the sheriff from behind, she dragged him to the water. The heels of his boots caught on the rocks along shore. She kicked his legs to dislodge him. Dropping his upper body into the water, she pushed the rest of him in by his feet. His belly bobbed above the surface as his legs sank. If only she had an apple to stick in his mouth. Jamie laughed. Tonight, Fuzzy would feed well on the meal she provided.

A thick mass of algae flowed from the cave, sliding beneath and around sheriff Anders. Kerplunk. They pulled him under. Bubbles burped from below. A few fatty flesh bobbers rose, then disappeared in little eruptions of green fuzz. Pieces of Fuzzy broke off and came back together, like the mercury she'd played with in science lab.

The water went still. The sheriff's bones and bits of cartilage were all that remained. Every soft bit had been devoured.

Fuzzy had grown again.

What would she do with the sheriff's vehicle? She couldn't disappear it like Mark's truck.

Images and whispers filled her mind. An accident. The fire would destroy most of the evidence, except for the bones. With them, the sheriff would be identified, and the whole incident would be declared a horrible tragedy. She'd seen it work in crime movies. No reason it couldn't work for her.

She'd put the bones in his vehicle, light it up, and push it over the cliff. No one would spend much time on the case. People out here were expendable. Usually, the last position anyone took was here, much like a retirement drop off. Out to pasture, and all of that. She giggled at the thought of the sheriff hanging from a hook at the meat market. That was a fitting fate after being pastured.

The forest floor was still plenty damp from the spring thaw, and the trees had fresh green growth. She wouldn't need to worry about it all going up in flames. She'd never take the risk if there was a chance of starting a forest fire. Never.

She'd need a few things from her cabin. Cloth, a lighter, maybe some fuel too. The Bronco wouldn't give her the spectacle she wanted without assistance. She'd have to do something with the bones in the meantime. She couldn't take the chance of an animal carrying one off. Human bones did tend to alert folks. Plus, she didn't want potential investigators to find any missing.

They'll be safe in the water. Clear as if she'd spoken it herself, yet it wasn't quite a voice, only a feeling, a sureness that she didn't question.

She rode back to her cabin and grabbed supplies. She didn't need much, an old blanket, her Zippo, and a magazine.

Back at the springs, Jamie fished out the sheriff's bones with a branch. She gathered them inside the blanket. Pulling the edges of cloth together, she slung the bone pack over her shoulder, and headed down the road to the sheriff's SUV.

She tossed the bones into the Bronco. Then she started it up and shifted to neutral. Tearing pages from the magazine, she lit them and threw them inside.

With help from her buck knife, she ripped a strip of cloth from the blanket. Going around the back of the SUV, she unscrewed the gas cap and stuffed the cloth inside, then lit the end.

The fire started slowly. Then, the wind howled, fanning the flames into a nice blaze. She moved to the rear of the vehicle and pushed. Inside the Bronco, the burning magazine pages caught the cloth seats, throwing sparks and wisps of flame into the cab.

She dug in, shoving with her full body weight. Gravel crunched as the Bronco rolled. She let the hill do the rest of the work. The sheriff's rig sailed over the cliff, landing with a thundering boom and crunching of trees. The explosion she'd hoped for didn't come. Instead, the fire ate methodically, leaping and sputtering upon the tires and popping a bright, albeit small, burst when the gas tank blew.

Billows of smoke rose from the crash. An orange glow lit the night. She waited a reasonable amount of time to have run down the hill from her cabin before calling dispatch. Then, she made that call.

Mandy picked up on the other end. With the appropriate amount of breathlessness, Jamie told her that a car had gone off the road.

"It's bad. Bring the fire department."

"You seen the sheriff? He was supposed to be heading that way," Mandy asked.

"No, you don't think—"

Mandy cut her off. "No, no, of course not. He should be there soon."

Jamie kept a shake in her voice, which wasn't too hard with the way her nerves were acting up. "Of course. I'll be here. Tell them to hurry."

The brush alongside the road rustled. Jamie stepped back, prepared to fight whatever emerged. Pepper spray at the ready, Jamie waited.

Aaron slunk out from behind the bushes, one eyebrow raised. Cool as the first snowfall.

"The sheriff, Jamie? What were you thinking?"

She'd completely forgotten about Aaron. Had he seen everything?

"I thought you were dead. Where were you?" Jamie thumbed the knife, rolling its handle in her palm.

"Whatever your plan is, it'll never work without me. If you help me, I'll go along with whatever you want." He looked down the road, sirens blaring in the distance.

"Yeah, of course," Jamie said.

She couldn't afford to argue with or kill him with emergency services on the way. From the sound, they'd be here any second. She didn't really want to kill Aaron, but she would if she had to. Nothing would get in the way of her getting back in the water.

The sirens grew louder.

"Well, we should probably go meet them, don't you think?" Aaron patted her shoulder and walked towards the fire engine's wails.

Jamie caught up and walked one step ahead, reminding Aaron of his place.

Rescue teams with ropes and climbing gear arrived shortly after the fire engine. Not much they could do until reaching the vehicle. By the time they got down to the Bronco, there wasn't much left to rescue.

They found the remains and transported the bag of bones to the forensics unit. Everyone knew what that would reveal. There was no mistaking the Sheriff's Bronco, even when burned and melted down to the frame. His blackened license plates were the final confirmation. Forensics were just routine.

Sheriff Lewis arrived.

"What the hell happened here? Sheriff Anders has been driving this road plenty long enough. Doesn't make any damned sense." She dabbed tears with her handkerchief, trying not to smear her eye makeup.

Aaron looked dutifully sad. "Deer maybe? Hard to believe he'd overcorrect like that. Not sure."

Jamie piped in, "We were in the shed, closing up for the night, when we heard him go off the road. Craziest thing. You don't think he'd been drinking?"

Ann shook her head. "Hope not. Must've been something, rigs ain't supposed to burn so easily. Not one I've ever seen."

Aaron showed the proper amount of disbelief and grief, even produced a few tears. Turned out he was an excellent liar. Jamie stared at the ground as if in shock. They'd all believe that reaction from a female, always underestimated by her appearance. In this case, it worked for her. No way she'd spill tears for that old bastard of a sheriff.

As she watched Aaron's act, she wondered again how much she didn't know about him. Might have to find out as soon as this mess was taken care of. The two investigators came over and completed the grieving circle. Jamie had never met them before.

The tall one had a notepad and pen. The shorter one shined his flashlight on the pad.

"My condolences. We're all pretty upset. I just need to ask a couple questions," the investigator said, pen poised.

"Happy to help any way we can." Jamie squinted, hoping it mimicked the sad expression on everyone else's faces.

Bats flew circles above, scooping moths, mosquitos, and whatever the night offered into their hungry maws.

The questions were standard. What did you see? What did you hear? That sort of thing. Mostly, everyone was trying to get back home. A tragic accident happened here. No reason for suspicion. They wrapped things up with pats on the backs, hugs, and condolences. Nothing new to see here. Until Aaron opened his mouth.

"Funny, I hadn't noticed these tracks before." Aaron toed the dirt with his shoe.

He had to be messing with her, but why would he do that?

Tracks, straight tracks with no signs of skidding to brake, led towards the cliff.

"We got pictures. Not quite sure what to make of it either, but we'll let the experts check everything out. Maybe, suicide," The tall one said.

The shorter one piped up, "We just do the initial assessment. We leave any conclusions to the forensics unit."

Jamie's lips twitched as she clenched her jaw, glaring at Aaron.

The tall one stuck his notebook in his pocket.

"Well, that should do us for now. Thanks all. Really sorry for your loss. Loss to us all, when it's one of ours."

The short one bowed his head.

Then the two investigators and Sheriff Ann headed out, leaving Aaron and Jamie alone.

"Sorry, Jamie. I just wanted to make sure they knew we were cooperating. The two of us are beyond suspicion if we were together, right?" It wasn't a question, but a warning. "I have a plan, a new trap, but it'll need to be placed inside the cave. Are you up for it?"

That was a death mission for anyone except Jamie, but Aaron didn't know she had communicated with Fuzzy. He didn't know that they'd become friends.

Maybe it was time she rid herself of Aaron. Doubtful he'd thought of that. He'd never suspect such a thing from her. Even though it grew more tempting all the time. It didn't matter. Aaron couldn't disappear before the authorities had closed their investigation. They'd want to talk to him again. She needed him to corroborate her story.

Jamie returned Aaron's grin, trying to make nice.

"We're going to wait for morning, so I don't get eaten before I get to the cave?"

"I'll bring the trap to the springs first thing tomorrow. You'll like it. Think we'll finally catch ourselves an algae eater." Aaron chuckled.

She hated his name for Fuzzy, especially now that she knew how wondrous they were.

"We should both get some rest." Jamie lifted her hat, repositioning it on her head. "Make sure you bring your bike in. Last thing we need is some kids taking off with it."

"I've got an idea for that, too. We'll make sure kids quit coming up here." Aaron pulled a rubber mask from his pocket. "Gonna start our own urban legend. Keep those kids away for good."

Jamie understood what he had in mind. Word would travel fast.

"Might just work, Aaron. Might just work." The corner of her mouth twitched upwards a bit. She still liked the kid, even when she was being manipulated by him. "See you in the morning, then?"

"You know it." Aaron pulled the mask over his head. In the dark, he looked like a strange ape. "I'll wait and watch."

"You gonna stay up all night?" Jamie asked.

"No, no need for that. I'm going down to them. To the main road. Let a few headlights flash off of me in the dark. Should be good enough to keep the kids away."

"You and I both know it'll only keep a few away. More will come to see the monster."

"I'll make sure they're going elsewhere for excitement."

"Need the truck?"

Now Jamie understood the complete picture. Aaron would set them off the path. How long had Aaron been doing this?

"Thanks, Jamie. We're a great team."

Jamie threw him the keys and headed back to her cabin. After all the excitement, she'd sleep like the dead tonight.

CHAPTER TEN

T he contraption Aaron brought to the springs the next morning looked ridiculous. The entire carcass wrapped in tinfoil with a tiny opening no bigger than a small twig between the two life vests attached to the bottom by bungy cords. She wasn't sure what kind of animal hid within. Didn't much matter as long as it was still warm. She wrapped a rope around the middle, letting a section hang free to tie off.

"All right, I'm going in." Jamie grabbed one end of the rope and pulled the trap into the water.

Aaron's smile couldn't get any bigger without breaking his face. He was definitely up to something.

"This one's good and fresh. It'll get them excited. When they enter to feed, it'll be dark inside. While they're feeding, we'll pull them into the light. They'll stay inside, in the darkness and we'll have them."

"Might work," Jamie mumbled. Fuzzy was much faster and stronger than Aaron seemed to think. That tinfoil would never hold them in.

She continued toward the cave and stepped through the opening with the trap. As soon as she entered the darkness, her mind filled with memories of her family. Her mother's bosom where she rested her tired head after a day working with Dad on the farm. The water, soft and warm and forgiving, just like mama. The colors and voices bright with rage like her father. Jonny's sweet smile and playful nature soaked into her. She'd spent a lifetime trying to make up for that terrible day. Finally, she'd found the warmth and love of family again.

Aaron was nothing like Jonny.

She placed the trap, barely aware of what she was doing. It took all of her will to leave the darkness of the cave. She couldn't stay, not yet.

Jamie waded out of the cave. "That should do it."

Aaron was gone. Why would he leave? What was that kid up to? He became more of a problem all the time. Stepping from the springs, the jagged rocks massaged her feet. Her body tingled with delight. The wind caressed her skin. Whatever Aaron was up to, she felt too good to worry about it now. She laced up her boots and went back to her cabin.

Trying to relax on the couch with the latest issue of Canadian Wildlife, her thoughts turned to Aaron. Where had he gone? Wherever it was and whatever he was doing it was no good for Fuzzy or her. She'd find out more about Aaron one way or another.

She hopped onto her bike and rode down to the parking area. He wasn't there. It was empty and quiet, with nothing but a bunch of tracks in the dirt from last night.

She rode to his cabin. The evergreens were full and bright, and birdsong filled the air. The mountains sparkled in the sunlight. Ah, she lifted her face to the sky, closing her eyes and allowing her bike to gently coast down his drive. She stopped by his porch. There was no sign of Aaron.

She knocked on the cabin door to be sure he wasn't home. Nothing. Looking around and listening for noises, she tried the doorknob. Locked. There wasn't much reason to lock doors out here in the forest. Bears hadn't learned to turn knobs, at least not yet. Why had Aaron locked it?

Giving the door a hard push with her shoulder, it swung open with a pop and creak. The stench reminded her of Jonny. What the hell had Aaron been doing in here?

She shut the door behind her the best she could. It hung a bit crooked on its hinges. Strange how easily she'd been able to break it down. She held her shirt over her mouth and nose. It didn't help much but was better than nothing.

Every bit of wall, except the one small window, was covered in newspaper articles and photos. She wasn't sure what they were all about, so she looked closer.

The news article on the first clipping was about missing children in a Peruvian jungle. The photo heading showed a cave with bones, piles of bones, scattered near the entrance. Another showed a large, silhouetted object standing between the trees. Too big for a human. The headline read "Proof at last! Yowie in the outback!" She walked along the wall. A lake with a floating dock, a dark oil slick of an object floating nearby. "Missing teens eaten by lake monster?"

One after another, she browsed the pictures and articles. Carcasses, remains, bugs of some sort, mentions of missing persons in different states and countries. Some in foreign languages. Several were so old and yellowed, the print had faded beyond readability.

Aaron was interested in urban legends, but this was a whole other level of bat shit crazy. He must have collected these since he was a kid. Or, maybe from his grandfather. Many of these were much older than Aaron.

Jamie walked through the cabin, examining photos and clutter. Aaron knew better than to let things go this way. Hundreds of empty nightcrawler containers and scattered dirt cluttered the floor. Vials, beakers, and a dozen or more small aquariums were arranged on the counters, interspersed with junk. A towering pile of bones filled the sink. A glint of silver caught her attention. On the counter lay a set of keys she didn't recognize. She picked them up. A key ring with the VW emblem hung through her fingers. The Volkswagen. What had he done?

Murky water filled three quarters of the small aquariums. In others, mice and rats scratched around in dirty substrate. What the hell was Aaron doing collecting mice and rats? And what were the bones? Jamie opened the fridge. Nothing but soda. What did he eat?

In one of the tanks, a mouse sat alone in the darkness of a hollow log. The rest of the tanks were packed full. A nose peeked out of the log. It was covered in blue-green fuzz. As Jamie moved closer, the nose tucked back inside. Only the shape of a mouse huddled in the darkness was visible.

Another aquarium filled with water sat beside it, a large magnifying glass attached to the front. Bending down, she peered through the glass. Little bits of algae floated in the water, blue-green. Almost the same color as Fuzzy. The mouse's nose was that very same color. An emptiness hollowed Jamie's belly, a yearning to smash all the tanks. Their emotions filled her but didn't satisfy her hunger. They were all Fuzzy.

A creature with huge teeth and fangs, dwarfing its tiny fins and tail, swam towards the glass, gnashing. Algae clung to it, obscuring its features, but under magnification the body within was revealed. The mice in the tank next to it scattered as it hit the glass. Bits of algae floated away, revealing its beige, roughened skin and tiny fins. These creatures were in some of the pictures. Not bugs, but some sort of fish.

Had Aaron been hunting them all along, following them, or had he planted them? Her body told her no. He studied them. They'd known him a very long time, and they hated him. He tried to control them. Their hate swirled with the darkest of indigos.

She peered through the glass of the next tank over. The entire front panel was magnified. They swam like tadpoles in a wriggling swarm, algae clinging to their skin. Without magnification, they appeared as nothing more than a fuzzy mass of blue-green. Fuzzy. This is what they were all along. All of them connected, a collective.

An engine cut off outside. Aaron. He must have taken the truck again. She'd been so distracted by the creatures that she hadn't heard him pull up. It was too late to get out and there was not much of anywhere to hide.

The bathroom door hung open. She stepped inside and slid behind the shower curtain. Jamie hoped Aaron's personal hygiene was as bad as his housekeeping skills, but if so, how did he manage to stay looking so good? Then, she noticed the bloodstains on the shower walls and floor, dried to a dark reddish brown. What was Aaron doing?

He'd know someone broke down the door. Maybe she should confront him and get this over with once and for all. She stroked her trusty knife.

The shower curtain was made of fabric, the kind you can see through from the inside but not from the outside. Aaron entered the cabin. He had a gun in his hand. Confronting him with a knife wasn't going to work.

He scanned the cabin with narrowed eyes, looking for her she assumed. Walking through the main room, he stopped at the tanks and picked a vial off the floor. She'd knocked it over in her haste to leave. He placed it back on the counter and walked towards the bathroom. She held her breath, clutching the knife.

Right before he entered, the radio went off. Every cabin had a scanner so the wardens would know what was going on and be able to respond to nearby situations.

"A Volkswagen Beetle has been reported out on Gramary road. No one around. Looks like it was vandalized," the dispatcher said.

Jamie didn't recognize the voice, but she didn't know all the dispatchers on the scanner's channels. Aaron stopped before entering the bathroom and went to the radio. He put on the headset.

"Not too far from us here. I'll check it out."

His back was turned. This was her chance.

She stepped from behind the curtain, standing behind the bathroom door, watching through the crack.

Aaron went back to the kitchen, stopping in front of the line of aquariums.

"How are my babies doing? Sorry I was late." He opened one of the mouse tanks and picked up a shiny black rodent by the tail.

He tossed it into the aquarium full of murky water. The Fuzzy engulfed the mouse. Within seconds, bones cleaned of flesh dropped to the bottom of the tank.

He turned, staring directly at Jamie through the door's crack. He stepped towards her. She prepared to fight. Aaron's arm pulled back, something in his hand. A metal canister hit the bathroom floor, and the door slammed shut.

Jamie choked and gasped. Her lungs burned in the thick chemical cloud. She tried to turn the doorknob, but she couldn't breathe. Gagging and coughing on fumes, pain overwhelmed her. Her body was on fire. Everything dimmed to a pinpoint and went black.

When she awoke, Aaron stood over her holding a vial and a syringe. There was a chain looped around Jamie's waist. The other end wrapped around Aaron's bed frame. Aaron stood just out of reach.

"Perfect. I was wondering how to get you here. Looks like you came to me. You've seen everything, right?" He nodded towards the counters.

"Why didn't you tell me about them?" She searched for her knife, but it was gone. "I thought we were partners."

"Ah, looking for this?" He held up the knife, twirling it in his fingers. "You weren't planning to use this on me, were you?"

His charming grin held an edge of contempt and hatred. God, how had she ever liked him?

Aaron walked back to the aquarium where he'd dropped the mouse. Pulling a syringe from his pocket, he dunked the end into the water and filled the vial with blue-green slime.

"I've tested a few animals but haven't had the opportunity to test humans yet. Not for lack of trying. Don't know why everyone has to put up such a fight. No good to me dead. Well, except as food that is." He laughed as he crossed the room.

"We make a good team. I can help you." She scanned the room for something she could use as a weapon.

Aaron stopped in front of her. "Oh, you are going to help. More than you know. More than you could in any other way."

"I can't disappear. They'll look for me." It was true, not that Aaron likely cared, but whatever it took to stall him.

Aaron laughed. "A lot of people have gone missing around here. Won't much surprise anyone when we disappear too. Maybe they'll think we were lovers and ran off together like two wild kids." He winked and stroked her cheek with his hand.

Jamie pulled away. "Don't touch me. No one will ever believe that."

Aaron took a step back. The smile fell from his face. "Don't be so sure. Even the sheriff mentioned the way you looked at me. Remind you of an old boyfriend? Is that it?"

She didn't want to satisfy him with an answer, but anything to stall him. She wasn't sure what his plans were for that syringe, but she was sure it wasn't anything good.

"My brother. You remind me of my brother. We were a good team too." She heard the Fuzzy in the tanks calling.

They didn't want to be caged. They wanted to join the others in the springs, so did she.

"We are a good team. We'll be even better once I've injected you with the source. That's what you found. The source of the cryptids. Or a particular type of cryptid, anyway. I've tracked and followed them for longer than I can recall. Swamp monsters. You're the only human I've seen infected. You're changing, Jamie. I know you feel it." Aaron stepped forward.

Jamie tried to get away, but he grabbed her arm. The needle pricked her shoulder, sending warmth across her chest.

"They live in the bloodstream and make their hosts voraciously hungry. That's my theory. We're about to find out for sure." Aaron smiled again, wide, and Jamie saw the fangs emerge through his gums as he laughed.

"You're—"

"Don't worry, I'm no swamp monster. Have yet to figure out exactly what I am or what created me. Might have been a bat got infected. Then, that bat bit me. Different animals exhibit the mutation differently, but nothing is as strong as one infected by the original. We are so fortunate to have them here."

Jamie's vision dimmed, becoming a single fine point where all she saw was Aaron's face, then she fell into darkness.

Chapter Eleven

Jamie awoke next to the steaming waters. Aaron was nowhere to be seen. That bastard was probably in the blind, watching. The perfect place to observe her from a distance. Now she was certain Aaron had built that blind in the first place. He had been assigned to this post shortly before she'd found it. He'd also been the one to convince her they could wait to clear it. Goddammed Aaron.

A deer carcass lay in the water, waiting like all the other animals she and Aaron had left as bait. It wasn't quite dark or the deer would already have been eaten. She wasn't sure what had happened to the foil trap she'd left. Aaron must have removed it. Fuzzy would never fall for Aaron's silly trap, but the deer was fresh. Jamie sniffed the air, warm blood. She was ravenous.

The trees around the springs rustled in the breeze, and the forest grew silent as the sun made its final descent behind the Three Sisters.

Fuzzy rolled out of the cave. Jamie would never see their multitude, too small for the human eye. All she'd see was the movement of their swarm, the mass of algae that clung to them, rippling before they devoured everything. But it didn't matter, she didn't need to see them anymore. She felt them, was them, and they were her. She had been blind. Her senses never truly awake until now.

Aaron had known all along. He'd plotted against her. Enslaved the Fuzzy. He wouldn't get away with it.

"Aaron? I know you're watching. I can still help if you let me in on the plan."

What was he trying to do? Why?

Aaron had talked about such voracious creatures, named many things in different places: vampire, wendigo, werewolf. Called different things throughout time. She'd never suspected the source of his cryptids would be these tiny, hungry, bug fish from the earth's crust. Hell, she hadn't believed any of it, let alone thought there might be a source.

The sound of gentle lapping at the shore filled the night. The crickets were silent. The water rippled and churned, alive with movement. She was the only one present, and she was hungry. Starving.

He'd put them inside her. She could feel them and hear their hum.

Flashes of ripping flesh and tendons, sucking blood from open wounds, and gnawing on bone. Had it been her all along? No, it was them. They were a collective, and she was now part of them.

How long had Aaron been doing this? Were there others like him? Others who helped the creatures spread? Was that what he was doing?

She, they, craved flesh, more flesh than she could ever consume on her own, but now she had help. She had Fuzzy.

Aaron. Don't forget Aaron. He had done this to her. It was all so clear now. All this time, they'd had help becoming something they never wanted to be. They wanted to be free but were stuck inside his cages, inside of her. They'd have to feed through her, with her. No. That was wrong. They were dying. Aaron had been wrong. Their death throes racked her body. She fell, writhing on the shore. She inched her way into the water to join them.

Their consciousness merged with hers. They soothed the dying and gave her calm. Together they devoured the deer. Its flesh warm from the steaming waters. The meat juicy. The blood divine. Her hands strong. Stronger than ever, as she ripped bone from tendon, gnawing on the deer leg like a drumstick on thanksgiving. Blood dripping from her lips and off her chin. Never had she felt such satisfaction.

They swarmed around her and with her. She forgot for a moment that she had a human body. Enveloped by the Fuzzy, she became part of it, eternally connected. She waited for death.

They pulled away without harming her. Moving like a wave, they slipped inside the cave, disappearing into a fissure in the rock. She wanted to return to the earth with the swarm, but her human body would not allow it. She settled back into a corner of the cave. Warm, dark, silent, and satiated, she nearly drifted to sleep.

An image of Aaron flashed in her mind. His little fangs and contemptuous smile. Her lips spread wide. Her tongue slid across her sharp pointed teeth. She licked her cheek to find smooth, hardened skin.

Swimming to shore, she exited the water. Her flesh chilled in the cool night air.

She lumbered towards the blind, joints stiffening, her hunger returning. Her movements slow, yet powerful. Each step, her bare, toughened feet left a shallow imprint as they shook the ground. When she arrived, the perch was empty. Aaron must have seen her coming. No way would he have missed the feeding.

She stalked through the night to his cabin. Her skin, a yellowish-green and covered in goose flesh, had become impenetrable. Rocks, pinecones, and sticker plants didn't slow her. The forest grew silent with her presence.

Her eyesight was sharp in the darkness, like permanent night goggles. All her senses on high alert. They'd been enhanced for nocturnal hunting. Fuzzy had changed her. She was hungry and cold. Freezing. Starving. Eating fresh meat was the only way to truly warm her. Yet she'd never felt more alive with desire. She had to find Aaron.

His bike leaned against his cabin. She stomped up the porch steps, grabbed the door handle, twisted, and pushed. The hinges splintered, cracked, and the molding pulled from the wall, releasing the door. She flung it aside.

Aaron whipped around, eyes wide, interrupting his haphazard throwing of clothes into a duffle bag. She smiled, lips closed, in the way she now realized he'd always smiled at her, like she had a secret, and it wasn't anything good for him. He backed up. Trying to gain his composure, his lip twitched but the smile didn't come.

"Jamie! You've found yourself. I hoped you'd come."

She opened her mouth wide, lips stretching until her face was little more than a hole with many rows of large sharp teeth. She clacked them together, nibbling on air.

Fuzzy called from their tanks, agitated. Angry they'd been imprisoned. Rage washed over her in waves of fuchsia and scarlet. She approached Aaron. He held up his hands.

"Come on, we're friends. All I've done is help. Look how magnificent you've become."

She wouldn't waste her energy responding. Closing in on him, she towered above, considering whether she might swallow his head in one bite.

He attempted to run, tendons swelling in his neck. She grabbed him by the throat with one hand, lifting him off his feet. His eyes bulged as his face turned purple. She slammed him against the wall. Articles and photos fluttered to the floor.

Then, he smiled. Fangs protruding, his body twisted and plumped. She lost her grip and stepped back in confusion. His skin had become leathery, membranes stretched between his limbs. He pushed her with so much force she hit the counter, knocking two aquariums to the floor. They shattered. Blue-green algae created an oil slick across the linoleum.

They cried out, but there was nothing she could do. She lunged for Aaron. He sidestepped, and she fell. She receded and Fuzzy filled her with swirling rainbows of fury.

Getting off the floor, the algae slick had moved. It was at Aaron's feet, slithering onto his shoes and up his bulky legs. He screamed and danced through the cabin, knocking junk off tables.

"You can't kill me! Nothing can!" He laughed hysterically, twirling and hitting the chair. Aaron, Fuzzy, and the chair landed in a tangle of limbs, chair legs, and blue-green fuzz.

Aaron's body covered in Fuzzy, they separated, leaving an opening for Jamie to feed. She jumped on him, ripping and tearing with teeth and claws. Letting their rage and hunger take over, they fed. Tiny wounds covered his skin, quickly growing larger and deeper, blood bubbling. The few scraps of clothes left disintegrating under millions of tiny teeth.

They tore off his arm. A fountain of blood squirted into the air. The arm twitched on the floor next to an article from the Kentucky Gazette and Aaron let out his last whimper. They gnawed his meat off the bone like it was kernels from a corncob at a summer picnic. Nothing but stringy bits left when they were done. Jamie laughed with them. Herself and Fuzzy, one and the same, together and separate simultaneously.

Her body warmed. Their fury lessened. The colors transformed to joy. They'd consumed all his soft parts. Her belly stretched taut like a pregnant woman about to deliver—reminiscent of the pictures she'd seen of quintuplet births. She rolled onto her back, resting a moment.

Lying on the floor beside the mess that used to be Aaron, her sense of fullness lessened. Her belly gurgled as it shrank, leaving her wanting. Goose flesh ran over her skin. She needed to get back to the water.

They slithered over and into her body. She was Fuzzy, blue-green, a walking bug-fish algae cluster. She couldn't tell where her skin ended, and the others began. She didn't care. It no longer mattered.

By the time they returned to the springs, she was ice cold. They were hungry. Always hungry. Eating was the only thing that would satisfy them, but the water helped.

As she entered the springs, warmth enveloped them in a coating of slimy welcome. Enough heat to keep off the chill. Wading, she dove beneath the steaming water and swam to the cave. A new world opened in turquoise and salmon. Fuzzy oozed through the fissure in welcome, engulfing her and the rest of them, one of many. They were all Fuzzy, and Fuzzy was all.

The sunrise had come, but it was dark in this safe space. They found a hot cubby hole to sleep in at the back of the cave.

When food came near, they would awaken and feed. There was enough for them all. No one would find Jamie among the rocks and algae. She wasn't alone, was never lonely; she had everything she wanted.

The only thing that might disturb her quiet were the screams of their meat, but those wouldn't last long. Fuzzy had grown and made quick work of their food.

She hoped the new warden appreciated a good soak.

About the Author

Roni Stinger lives in the Pacific Northwest, USA, where the moss and ferns hide magic and secrets. Stinger enjoys exploring new worlds with her characters.